THAT NIGHT

S.I.S.M.O.

DJS (YUVRAJ)

Made with ♥ on the Notion Press Platform
www.notionpress.com

S.I.S.M.O.

Contents

Prologue

The incident took place after the **DEAD BITE** two months ago.

CHAPTER I

Randy was blabbing about his and Keith's sensual experience that took place years ago to Dominik.

9:30 PM.

After exactly 9:59 PM on the clock, Randy's duty would be over and he'll go to his room on the 5th floor from the top.

It was the second of January, almost a month before Dom's birthday. Dom or Dominik was sitting on his wide and luxurious couch. Randy, still speaking about his sexual experience, had both his hands behind him and was standing in a formal bodyguard look behind the couch. Black coat, pants, tie, etc. Dominik was typing something on the laptop while Randy was still speaking. "Sir, are you listening?" Randy asked. "Ah, yes-yes. Tell me more!.." Dominik tried to appear as excited as possible. "Okay," replied Randy normally.

Meanwhile, Sylwia was passing by but stopped when she heard Randy saying, "Sir, please take care you won't tell this to anyone...because I needed to tell the secret to someone whom I can trust." "Don't worry. Randy, this would not skip my lip." He confirmed. These words caught her ears and she couldn't resist listening to what they were talking about. Tipping top quietly like a ninja she swiftly hid behind some wide curtains to quietly listen to them without coming into their field of vision.

"You know what happened?"

"What?" Dom said as he stood up and turned towards his room.

"What happened, tell me too." Since she couldn't hear clearly, Sylwia bumped and stood beside Randy with a smile like a small kid.

"Ugh..!" Dominik jumped in surprise and turned around. He saw Sylwia standing beside the couch with Randy. She was dressed in all white- *White full-sleeve T-shirt, and pants.* "Where did *she* come from?" Asked Randy sternly. "I don't know. Where did you come from 'Zuzanna'?" Asked Dom turning his laptop off after saving his business files.

A nickname by which Dominik calls her.

"I just happened to pass by when I heard Randy saying something like *don't tell anyone* and I came here. What are you both talking about?" She asked joyfully, deepening her voice at Randy's part.

She is mature in her behavior but starts behaving like a kid when it comes to midnight. Means she's sleepy...

"Tell me about it too!" She continued.

"Won't tell you..." Randy replied normally with a stern expression constant on his face. "Why?" She demanded. "B-Because it's a boyz talk," Dominik confirmed. "Boy's..?" "Yeah, you can't hear that!" Randy said again with the same expression. "But-But I won't tell anyone about it." She frowned and pinched her neck as a swear. She looked so desperate. "What the hell? Do you want to know the boy's stuff? I am surprised!" Dom was really surprised. "Wait, that means I can't hear that!" "Is that a question to be asked?!" Dom was surprised at how childish can one be. "Go! Go!" Exclaimed Randy at her pointing his head in the direction she came from while his hands were still joint at his back. She pouted sadly looking at Randy with resentment and started moving. "What is this girl?!" Randy started when Sylwia just started to move. "Calm down Randy. She's probably just sleepy. She's so childish when sleepy you know. Sometimes..." Dom's voice was unruffled.

"You both are bad boys. Not telling me anything..." Sylwia stood at her place and said.

That was quite like Hannah's statement.

When *she* behaves childishly of course...

"What the hell?" Dom exclaimed as he turned around back to her.

"You wanna hear the story about the boys right? Come I'll tell you!" Randy yelled at her gravely. Sylwia didn't move a bit at the statement but hesitated to come. She didn't take a step ahead. Randy repeated the exact statement to her again and she walked away quietly as if nothing happened. "What are these adamant minds, sir?!" Randy complained after she left. "Let go, let go. She's just sleepy didn't I already tell?" Dominik suggested quietly. Nonchalant Dominik nature is back! He was concerned about his high-power behavior during the **Dead bite reaper** mission. Randy started the narration of his story again but another distraction came to happen.

"I am back! (Laughs)" 8 entered the hall again with the same sarcastic wide grin on his face, as his habit, and Hannah was also with him. She was in a green crop top and shorts while 8 was in a simple vest and blue shorts. They both were smiling.

"Sir. I think that I'll be telling the rest of it sometime later. Maybe tomorrow?" Randy didn't want his story to be spread to everyone.

"No. Some other day."

'Perve Randy.' Thought 8 in his mind as his behavior to tease Randy about being bisexual. Not good to be honest, but 8 remains adamant about manners.

"I think it's already 10:00 so I shall go now."

"Alright." Dominik approved and Randy walked out of the room.

"What happened?" Asked Hannah.

Same question as Sylwia.

"Nothing happened Hannah. It's 10:00 already didn't you hear sister? Go, go to sleep now." *'Damn you 8. Randy walked away without completing his duty hours. Cause he knew you could make him go mad and rageous again like you always do by your comments to him.'* Dom brooded staring at 8 who was standing and smiling at the Zeus statue among the many greek gods statued in the hall.

"Nobody likes him right?"

Dom nodded to him in reply and moved his eyes from him to the phone screen that said 9:45 PM.

NIGHT AT 11:42 PM:-

8 was laying on his back on the bed with his dark hands wide and the portion from his navel till his legs were covered inside the white blanket. Toes were out too. *'I want to pee.'* he thought to himself while his eyes were wide open staring at the ceiling.

He must be feeling lazy for getting up from the warm bed to the dark and cold outside. His room temperature was cool and he was laying in the best position possible. The moon lamp's yellow light seemed more comfortable inside his room. It was a huge discomfort to get up. The comfort was unavoidable, yet he has to break that since it already was quite a while now. #No_luck.

He walked from his room towards the hall. The hall was glowing with dim yellow lighting. The contrast with white-washed walls and all the luxurious stuff and furniture combined look really pleasant to the eyes. Like a royal suite!

That was Alice's, so-called boss of the mansion, idea to keep the mansion glowing during the night.

This is a Trillionaire family. This works under the jurisdiction of Alice, Dominik, and Hannah. However, most of the money is actually in the form of their business shares. *That much for this part.*

Anyway.

8 close the door behind him and walked towards the kitchen first.

'पहले पानी पी लेता हूँ मैं उसके बाद जाऊंगा,' he thought which means- I drink water first. I'll go after that, 'बहुत मजा आएगा!' The thought- *'Would be so much fun!'*, rose a momentary grin on his face.

While drinking from the glass, something happened.

A dark figure dashed somewhere from the left side towards the hall. At least he assumed so... Wasn't too sure but, it wasn't fast though, more like a normal person than a paranormal entity. It took a full 2 second time to do the whole action... maybe 1*ena half* as 8 observed it. And appeared as a formal movement.

But it still was enough to shock someone at night times.

CHAPTER II

8 did show some amount of consciousness of amusement towards it, but just like in any typical horror movie, he ignored it at first and started towards his room again.

While passing through the hall he came to know that that wasn't something he had imagined so wild, but it rather was a physical reality!! Someone. **Not a Ghost,** but a good heightened man. 8, or Shreyance Mani by name, tried to figure out who he was. "Hello, I am all up. Yeah,..waiting... Should I? Okay coming out!" Said the man to the person on the phone and *put that in his left pocket with his right hand,* just a habit 8 thinks he knows of someone and stood in front of the suite door. "लेल्ले-उल्ले? वह आधी रात को क्या कर रहा है? वह करना क्या चाहता है?!" 8 murmurred that means- (*His unique quote*)? What is doing at midnight? What does he want to do?!

Though Dominik talked in a very low voice, the tone and density of his voice and hairstyle helped 8 in recognizing the person. The ghost he saw was nonother than Dominik. The same Dominik who will be turning 18 next month (since he was concerned about his age in New York during the reaper case). 8 was standing behind the white curtains, as Sylwia did, to cover himself from being revealed.

Who was on the phone Dominik was talking to? Why did he run through the hallway? Dom twisted the door knob and ran out through it immediately in a hurry. The *automatic door knob* that was described in the **TRILLIONAIRE'S**

NIGHT RIDE.

Anyway.

"इ(वह) इतनी दरे रात मेंजाग रहा हैरे..!(He's waking up so late at night..!)" 8 murmured to himself in the silence of the atmosphere after the footsteps faded. "क्या मझुे उसके पीछे जाना चाहिए?(Should I go after him?)"

Should he?

He was a bit brooding upon the thought. But his curiosity won over the negative feelings. With a bit of resentment but much curiosity, he decided to look for it.

8's half drank water glass was still on the kitchen slab and he forgot to pee too and ran out of the door to solve the mystery.

He entered the hall covered by the same dim lighting. Glancing at both sides he saw Dominik walking away at a far distance from him with an additional black hat upon his head. Just like some fantasy character? Well, *Tokyo Ghoul* doesn't have anything similar; neither does *Sherlock Holmes* he's been reading for quite a while now. But Holmes has a deerstalker cap. Anyway, a black hat at the head followed by a black, shiny clock beneath it tied to the neck and black, shiny boots. Making *taps...* on the floor echoing and dying immediately. 8 almost felt like he was seein' some detective out of the fantasy walking away from him on his mission.

MISSION? He felt himself to be living in the same fantasy. A detective following a detective.

Could Dom be on a mission!? But late at night? Impossible.

Akiraaa...(He thought blushing.)

"WTF! Focus Shreyance, Focus. No time for love. वह वहाँ गया!(He went there!)" 8 jogged and followed him, maintaining a safer distance on his tip-toes, and jumped behind a square-shaped table seeming thing with a white flower vase on its top to hide as Dom had been moving his head to the back momentarily to ensure no one's following. The flowers were light yellow. Lily's favorite color.

Dominik, the being followed detective, had stopped at the stairways and took out his phone with his right hand from the left pocket, **habit**, and threw his head back with the phone stick to his right ear. He was staring at the corridor he came from- "Hello. Come fast, I don't have all the time in the world! It's a trouble. I may get caught you know."*'Trouble!?'* thought 8 while he was still in the hiding and keeping him in view by momentarily staires with stern eyes. Moments after a huge bodybuilder, black in skin color and huge body came to him from downstairs. He had a line-up haircut and, any bodyguard's requirement, black glasses on his eyes.

"You took quite a while," Dom's first greeting to him. "Come on. This small operation must be finished at once." "My apologies sir, come." Replied the huge-muscled bodyguard and showed Dom the way and they both jogged downstairs following the same direction through which the bodyguard himself came. "इ करना क्या चाहता है? पता लगाना होगा!(What does he want to do? I have to find out!)"

Even after going downstairs, 8 kept himself very sturdy and quiet. To be hidden of course.

The bodyguard and Dominik, as 8 saw them, went inside a bar through the wide glass door reflecting the bright lights from inside, and heard loud music which went quiet as death as the gates closed after their entry.

CHAPTER III

One thing to remember is that the mansion also consists of bars, nightclubs, and massage senators on each floor in the middle floor part of the mansion(For butlers, maids, and bodyguards whose working hours are during the day time) so to keep them relaxed during the off duty hours. They can enjoy all these luxuries like they would have in real life, with their friends and colleagues. For the nighttime workers, this follows vice versa...

To gain more clarity about the mansion and to the fullest of all the SISMO characters of this novel, please consider reading the 'TRILLIONAIRE'S NIGHT RIDE'. ↙

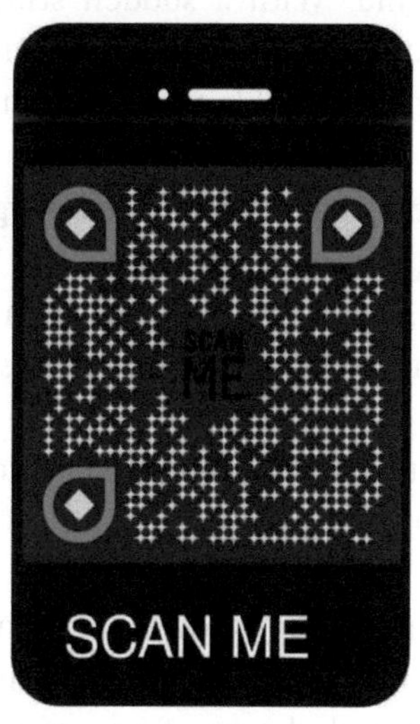

Most men go to such places for alcohol and pole dancers. Though there are limits set by Alice, Dominik, and Hannah(The leaders of the mansion) for the bars they've made. Still, it's in *the mansion, Dom's residence! He always appears unruffled to such places. Though he may drink light alcohol to relieve the mind, but it's with us he drinks..! Could it be possible he goes to his bars to enjoy himself? Alcohol! Girls!? He may appear uninterested, but still, could he, in reality, actually be fancying it? Saving one of his faces from us..? While all of us are asleep!?* All these thoughts 8's his mind instantly as he saw them going inside. Same at that moment.

'Cheating on Sylwia!' 8 has a habit of making things too quickly in his mind. With a sudden stimulation, he ran down the stairs toward the way of the bar and stood in front of the glass door, clearly able to see everything happening inside.

The disco lights, male and female bodyguards, dancing, drinking, talking in groups, gossiping, etc. Wide smiles on their faces and laughs. A DJ standing in the middle on a small platform playing disco music. *Disco music?* Yeah, must be.

8 wasn't able to hear anything from inside.

Some beautiful waitresses and bar girls were also doing their jobs.

8 tried and succeeding made his way inside the bar, he conceal himself perfectly. (**S.I.S.MO. training** of course) After he hid in the darkness of one of the tables inside,

closest to the exit he entered from, his eyes ran to find Dominik. *'He must be a perve and strippers his girlfriend.'* He was still thinking independently on his own without knowing much about the situation.

But what *was* the situation?

What was happening?

CHAPTER IV

Among the whole crowd of the many bodyguards, there was but one fellow who was dancing like a crazy madman with the other ones who were dancing normally. Drunk for sure. "इ(वह) कैसे नाच रहा है(How is he dancing)," he stifled a laugh. "कतिना गंदा लग रहा है...(He's lookin' so bad)" He continued and laughed again. The music was loud inside with the disco lights changing their colors momentarily. Heavy disco music fills the air like a sin party.

"Where are they? It's already so late, almost midnight!" Dom said to the same bodyguard. "Sir, they'll be here anytime now." The guard replied after checking his wristwatch.

"वे कसि बारे में बात कर रहे हैं..?(What are they talking about..?)" 8 couldn't hear the conversations between Dom and the guard. He observed them talking but couldn't decipher their lip movements and that was buzzing him even more. He was so suspicious of them. The fact that the bodyguard checked his wristwatch, his suspicion, by the SISMO training, grew even more and he rolled out of the table, intention to camouflage he knowingly blends himself into the big dancing bodyguard crew afterward. Nobody had noticed him since they were minding their own business. Some bodyguards were also sitting at the tables with bar girls in lingerie.

Anyway.

8 made his way through the crowd, keeping Dominik and the *big man* in view, and leaped for a safer place to maintain a view constant upon them. A minute later, he

found himself standing in front of the same crazy dancing guy. He was still dancing, even crazier. 8 finds that he's visible from there to Dominik and could be caught anytime if he did something stupid. "Oh shit! I must hide! He must be waiting for a pole dancer! I must record this whole thing to show the true face of *finicky Dominik* to everyone," His eyes were stern at both of them. "I must gather proof."

Look at this guy...here 8 was able to steal from the crazy dancing guy his cell phone furtively. This was one of the special abilities he learned from the SISMO training. *Thief in disguise.*

After finding himself a comfortable place to hide he unlocked the phone(since it had no password) and started recording Dominik at that very moment, hiding behind the green curtain and lying down himself to keep himself hidden from them but focused the camera on himself first. Laying on the ground made him camouflaged in a much better way- "Yo guys!" he started in low voice in the middle of the music. "Here I am back with another brand new video guys and here I want to show you something really surprising guys... Just take a look, yo-yo!" He switched to the back camera and started recording Dominik with thc smartphone. Dom was being recorded from the back, sitting at the table while the face of the *big man*was clearly visible. Dom appeared to be a detective by his outfit, to be precise, and has covered his face too with his big collars and could not be recognized that 8 confirmed in the video just a moment ago.

8 is a famous vlogger cum YouTuber, and for this video, he was making it like a vlog by adding dialogue to it. Habitually...

"We can't just suddenly outrage at it."

"I wonder what would be everybody's reaction if they find out that the leader of this mansion, me, is sitting among them, secretly. Concealed, and observing them." Said Dom with a suspicious smile at the man.

"They'll be surprised seeing you, sir. THELEADER OF THE HOUSE in his own bar."

"Absolutely."

Meanwhile.

"Yo, guys!!" Started 8 adding irrelevant dialogues for fun. "Yo! Yo! Yo! Do you hear that guys? I knew it! I always knew that Dominik was a trickster and was betraying us...Yo, can you believe this guys?"

At the end of 8's dialogue, Dom saw, from the glass gate came, Randy inside the bar as well with a goonish grin on his face. He walked towards the dancing committee and sat beside them on one black table. Smiling and enjoying looking at their dance while on the other hand, Dom clapped two times and a waitress walked up to him and placed two glasses of, what looked like water.

"Wonder what Randy's doing here." Dom took a sip of the drink from the glass.

"But for what reason sir? He's off-dutied, right? He can go around in all the bars and massage senators he wants."

"That's not what I am talking about Abayomi. The thing is that there are six clubs on each floor in the middle part. Each of them is similarly enjoyable, but he's in *this* particular club. Why? This doesn't seem normal to me. Why did he choose this particular club on the **lower** floor? Maybe because this is the closest to the stairs from both that go up and down. But this still bugs me."

"Maybe because he fought with someone...on the upper floor? You know him, sir. Since he's one of your personal bodyguards you must be aware of how fierce he is."

"No. *Possibly not true.* There are still five more bars from his floor, **upwards!** But while having so many choices, he chose to come down. Plus, if there were any fighting then you know, Abayomi, that the managing committee is aware that I am up to something right now. They would have informed me immediately. Since there's nothing popping up on my phone I am suspecting this."

"You're suspecting your own bodyguard?"

"No. But possibly yes...there must be something. For now, Abayomi, where are our most trusted men for this case? Call them..."

Abayomi started to call again and went toward the washroom. Dom is still in the same spot on the camera.

'We are having some disguised agents for this matter as well. So, could it be that you are one of them too, Randy? Is it?' Dom pondered upon the possibility.

"Yo, guys," 8 turned the camera to himself. "YO! YO! YO! Do you see that? He must be going to do something eighteen plus, you know what I am talking about guys. The bodyguard went to the bathroom! Dominik's too concealing it from us! I'll bust him, guys. If you are enjoying my video then please let me know in the comments! Also, check out my new Bugatti printed merge guys, and also like this video, subscribe if you are new, and comment down below- ***#BustedfinickyDominik.*** Yes, guys..!" He turned the camera back to Dom, enjoying making the video so much!

"Please give me one more glass of water."

"Sure sir." Replied the waitress to Dominik and handed it over to him.

"Yo, guys..," 8 was shocked. "He must be consuming more alcohol guys!! Yo! The word 'WATER' must be a secret code for alcohol. *I can see some bubbles in it guys..!*"

Meanwhile in the background, Randy was taking sips of the pineapple ginger beer. He saw Dominik but couldn't recognize him because of his disguised outfit. Though first, Randy appeared to be finding out about the unrecognizable person under the big coat but seeing that *Big Abayomi* was talking to him he wasn't too concerned.

Must be some man freezing or some other reason. Well, what should I care, Big Abayomi is talking to him. Must be a bodyguard or some other worker. Wow, they danced really well!

Everything except Dominik seemed normal.

One thing to remember is that 8 didn't see Randy entering the place and so he was unaware of his presence. He started from his rest position and fluently walked across the bar. Don't think he's taking another position for recording the proof with a different angle but the reason is far more serious. He paused the recording, put it on his table, and went to the washroom because he couldn't control it anymore. He needed to go. **He needed to pee.** Similarly, the drink that Randy just had reacted inside his body and he needed to go too. He needed the washroom so badly. Within a couple of seconds, Randy entered the washroom with 8 inside.

Both are unaware of each other at first.

CHAPTER V

8 hadn't planned to post the video publicly, but just to share it with friends and the members of the house. On friend's group to be precise. It is a private Social media group of some of the friends from Sky Will's Academy. All the friends at the *Night Ride* are added to the group, along with *Himawari* and *Mack*. 8's plan was simple. He sends the video to his phone first somehow from the phone he had stealth and then from his phone to the group with no effort. And finally, undo it from the dancing guy's phone deleting his number as well. Easy peasy lemon squeezy.

Anyway.

The inside of the gents' toilet was nothing special. Just as decent as any hotel. How it looks could be anybody's guess.

Well, why not?!

It's a mansion.

Both the boys, by coincidence, came out of the WC at merely the same time! Randy came out from the left restroom while 8 was just washing his hands. Yeah, he washes his hands sometimes too... When they both encountered each other, Randy started to rebel against him after some gestures of surprise. "Wa..? How?! What are you doing here?! Who let you in?" Despite he was drunk, his consciousness remained under control and his voice was still as coarse as ever. He pulled his collar with both his hands.

"I just..came in. It's,...my house too..." 8 replied. His voice stammered and he felt like time had stopped for him.

"No! I know you're lying," Randy yelled again. Randy's full description has been completely elaborated in the Trillionaire's Night Ride.

"You're lying! You're not an innocent one. I know you. I know that you wouldn't have come here without planning anything to create a riot! Tell me!" His strong voice echoed in the washroom. "रे..." 8's *thin* voice stammered again, in fear as he felt Randy's grip tightening on his collars even more. He felt his collar been crumbled inside the hot, raged palms. Randy's face turned red. 8 couldn't take his eyes off Randy's scary face. He felt his breathing. He could hear it and it was so heavy. Even the loud music being played outside could not fill the silence of the interior of the washroom.

What to do?

What to do?

What to *do..?*

"I am on a mission." 8 revealed to him his absolute intentions after taking a long pause. *Mission?* Randy couldn't get it.

Mission?

What was he talking about? Randy got confused at first but, after cogitating for some time he forged at him again. "Don't lie to me," He said. "I know this's just another play by your side. I won't leave you to create chaos here! Look, tell me your intentions already. Cause if it came up to me then-"

"This mission is a secret one. A-and should not be disclosed to anyone under any circumstances. **It is S rated!**"

"<u>Quick knowledge for you:-</u>

For SISMOS, they rate their missions according to the degree of importance and danger associated with it. In simple words and straightforward

- *if the mission is dangerous, then it is rated as X,*
- *if the mission is very dangerous, then it is rated as XX,*
- *and if the mission is extremely dangerous, then it is rated as ZZZ.*

Similarly,

- *if the mission is some special kind that can be disclosed but can be disclosed after its completion it is rated with S,*
- *the one which must be disclosed only if very nessassory as SS*
- *and which must be treated as being forgotten (must never be revealed) as SSS*

And in case the mission is both dangerous and secretive at the same time it can be rated as SZ(since S comes before Z in the alphabet). The number of Ss and Zs can vary based on the degree."

"Who do you think you're fooling, huh? I know you! And I am gonna kick your ass out of here." Randy took a long pause and said, not believing him. His furious nature was ever-increasing. 8 couldn't take it anymore. **He was missing content.** Randy was being an unnessassory evil. He was coming in between his work. And what was *he* doing here? It's not the floor allotted to him... Gotta do something. 8 forced his fingers into his nose grooves, deeply.

"AAH!" Randy groaned in pain and ran outside the washroom in full anger to catch 8, since he already had run away after doing the unexpected action, at any cost to demand the answers from him. He had many questions in his mind and that was obvious.

That was unexpected seeing 8 in a bar suddenly on one random night.

Randy himself was in the bar on the lower floor, but 8 *was in* the bar is more suspicious.

8 ran out of the bar but Randy had no clue about it. He was still thinking that 8 is still hiding somewhere inside the bar. Behind something maybe? He searched for him with stern and sharp eyes.

Meanwhile, 8 was running away from the bar while filming himself running in the camera.

He was still talking to it. "Yo! Guys... You know what guys? You won't believe what happened... What I am about to tell you guys is so unexpected!! His guards attacked me, guys! Yes, his guards attacked me..! I was about to die, he was about to kill me... Ugh..,(Clears throat) But I'll go inside again for you guys." He said and stopped to gain his breath back to normal.

CHAPTER VI

"Oof, damn you, Akira," Hannah came out of her room to grab a glass of water too. "She says that she wants to drink water however she's been sending me outside in the cold. I told her to keep a jar in the room. Don't I feel cold?" She complained to herself while passing through the hall with Greek god statues. Hannah was sleepy but went towards the kitchen to grab a bottle. While through her route she didn't see anything unexpected or to brood upon but one thing that showed its effect in the kitchen. There was a glass of half drank black water on the top of the slab, and on her way, she saw Shreyance's door ajar with a moon lamp's glow inside the room. Leaving the room like this and leaving the glass of water on the slab, were 8's traits. But she thought that 8 might be in the washroom. The distance from her bedroom to the kitchen was not much wider but the fact that she spent more than three minutes in the kitchen doing the whole thing(eating late-night snacks after giving Akira some water) and when she returned she saw that the door was still open made her worried. His favorite stuffed monkey was also inside the room, resting on the bed. *'What? Nobody spends time such as long as three minutes inside the washroom. Especially at midnight... Where is 8?'*

She tried to figure something out. Where he might be?

She mused hard on the thought but didn't come up with anything. Well, of course. How could she have known?

She tried to wake Akira out but that didn't help. **Didn't help.** She's asleepyhead, to be praised. "うーん、ママはあ

と2分お願いします...(Mmmm. Mumma please 2 minutes more...)" she says every time Hannah lands soft movements on her body to wake her up. She tried a few more- two, three, four times; but didn't help.

Sleepyhead...

Hannah knocked on Somchai's door as well and nevertheless, replies were heavy snores from the inside. Finally, she banged on Hiroshi's door and that resulted in her success. "What is it?! (yawn)" Hiroshi was rubbing his right eye and was standing under the door frame of his room, looking so sleepy and tired. "Something strange had happened..." and she explained everything to him.

"What? Missing..?" Hiroshi was so nonchalant about the talk;

"I mean he's not on the floor at all..." While on the other hand, Hannah appeared super anxious.

"Oh..."

"And I am going to look for him. I think I should!"

"Washroom?"

"I'd checked all but non of them were full."

"All of them?"

"Entirely. All the doors were open. And in all the suites."

"Then maybe he's sleeping with somebody."

"I don't think so. His phone and his *bobo* are in his room." (The stuffed monkey.)

"No, I don't have a good feeling about it." Hiroshi knew 8 more closely than Hannah. He knew that 8 is a troublesome kind and nothing bad could happen to him. He's the troublemaker. But Hannah was very kind to everyone who cared for him.

"Why?"

"I don't want to look for that バスタード(Basterd)."

"He's not in his room!"

"God! He must be somewhere inside the premises then. What do I care where he is?"

Their argument went on for a while but ended up with Hannah's victory Hiroshi had to agree to her and they went for it. Nobody can beat girls in arguments, personally.

"Great! Change quickly and we'll go for it! Okay!"

"Fine." Replied Hiroshi in low voice.

They both went inside their rooms to change their clothes while the suite went as quiet as death. Meanwhile, *the second detective*(8) returned to his room again, and after some moments he went out to the bar. As he left, Hiroshi came out, properly dressed for the night. After a couple of minutes, Hannah came out of her room too.

Properly dressed for the night..?

Well, maybe a bit overdressed for such a small matter...

CHAPTER VII

Hannah was dressed in a black leather jacket and a short top under it. *Her neck was equipped with a chain, darkish synthetic jeans, and black and shiny boots. Besides clothes, she had applied red lipstick and a bit of whitish makeup.*

For Hiroshi, he was wearing a red T-shirt with a brown jacket over it. A gadget bag hanging to his neck containing survival weapons and tools provided by the SISMO(Though no requirement, it's Hiroshi's style), and moving forward for the bottom were black jeans and hideous and torn brown boots. His old boots that her mom bought on the month of Sundays, telling him that he can wear them in the future for a long time after he grows up.

"Everything's fine still, what is it you are carryin' with yourself?"

"Ugh," Hiroshi started with a frown. "It's weaponry and rest tools. I know it's hideous to carry it for something like this, but why take a chance? Who knows what 8's up to *now*..."

"True that."

"How about you? Are *you* carrying something with you??"

"Umm...Yeah, I have lipstick, chopsticks, spray paint, socks, tissue, mosquito repellent, sunscreen, and some of my clothes. In this bag, see..." Hannah seemed so happy with the choices of items she had. Hiroshi's eyes grew wider. Knowingly it was Hannah's childish behavior because she was sleepy.

"You know it's night time right?" Said Hiroshi after a long pause.

"Umm, I don't know what's the point of taking these on a mission but I just found these things in the bag I carried with me."

"So you do have something with yourself which could be suitable for the mission?"

On this statement, Hannah went for her pocket inside her leather jacket and put out a pair of knuckles. "It's been long since I used my aesthetic knuckles..." Hannah sounded much wiser and more intense with a confident smile. **No, Hannah's not in the mood to play!**

• • •

8 entered the bar. Disco lights crossed his eyes as well as he realized the same place full of beer, dancing bodyguards, beautiful bar girls in lingerie, and a lot of fun. **Yet everything is within a limit.**

Dominik was at the same table as before but with someone new. A new bodyguard. Buzz cut, skinny, and had his hands crossed in his sitting position. He had fully rested his body in his chair. *Bigman,* Abayomi, was still in the same position provided he was checking up on his wristwatch repeatedly while Dominik seemed calm. 8 leaped for the same hiding spot, beware of Randy, and lay in the same position on the ground, shadowed because of the curtains. "अब बेटा, मैं तुम्हें दिखाता हूं कि मैं क्या हूं(Now son, I'll show you what I am.)"

He gave a small continuation intro to the video and started taping all three of them while they were murmuring something in a low voice. But the recording this time was with his phone. He had already sent the video to his phone and dealt with the original video from the other one, deleting his number too.

"Where is she? Why is she taking too much time?" Questioned Dominik with resentment.

"She's on her way, sir. 'Lumi' would be here anytime now I guess."

"रे," 8's focus intense as he heard about one more person. "Yo, guys. Do you hear? He talked of some Lumi girl, maybe his secret girlfriend; देख रही है सिल्विया?(You're seeing it, Sylwia?)" He said in a funny tone of voice.

"Sir. I've talked to her. She'd be here pretty soon then we could start." Said the thinner bodyguard after he hung up the phone. Dom nodded. "All right. Let's end this. Once and for all..." His voice intensified.

'रे? ऊ का कइल चाहत बा?' 8 thought in his regional language(What does he want to do?). For instance, he thought that it was not what he was thinking about but rather something of real importance. But he had to continue the vlog. "S-so you can see this, guys. This is his connivance with the 'Ostrich' and the 'Hippo' seeming bodyguards! They are planning a gambling party for the night, guys, and the winner will get a girl named Lumi... Um, yeah. सिल्विया देखो, देखो...(Look Sylwia, look...)" He continued his hypothesis with the so-called vlogging. Randy passed by meanwhile in front of Dom's table. Randy glanced at them, especially at Dominik who was in disguise. But since his mind was filled up with 8's recent memories, all he focused on was his search. He was so irritated.

Meanwhile, 8 started to shiver in fear since he witnessed Randy still searching for him and passed by him from very near. He knew that since he was in hiding, chances of him being caught were minimal, but his momentary shivers did add a shakey effect to his vlog. Maintaining that he continued to vlog...

Hiroshi and Hannah made their way through the hall and entered the corridor.

"Let's go." Said Hiroshi when his hands were on the doorknob. Hannah swallowed heavily and nodded with an intense expression on her face. He twisted open the lock and wide opened the door;

"Do you wish to use the washroom?" A manly voice suddenly greeted them in the hall. Hiroshi and Hannah jumped in surprise.

"Oh! Hannah, ma'am." The bodyguard bowed in front as he realized that Hannah was there too.

Both Hiroshi and Hannah still had their eyes flung open but despite that Hannah shaking that off started- "I was just thinking about taking a night round on my floor since I wasn't feeling sleepy and wanted to check how your guards are working, and Hiroshi needed to *pee*. So we both came out at the same time." She lied to her nerves but made the lie look as realistic as possible since she said it with full authority.

The guard stared at them for quite a while and replied- "Better not to do this ma'am. It's not as safe as it always was." A clear-cut reply.

CHAPTER VIII

The night bodyguard stood like marble, a statue, blocking their way in front of them with a stern expression. His body language looked as stern as the statues of greek gods inside. Hiroshi and Hannah exchanged glances. "But why?"

"Well, it's just an order ma'am. And I am neither supposed to tell who gave the order nor what the matter to concern is. I would like you, Hannah, ma'am, to return to your room," the guard replied. "And for you, Hiroshi sir, please go to the washroom and return fast."

"You're scaring me," Said Hannah to his reply.

"Not wanted to do that ma'am. I apologize, but we are here for your safety hence no need to worry."

"Drop the formalities; nobodies here. And tell us the whole matter. What happened?" Said Hiroshi.

The bodyguard at Hiroshi's statement moved his head to the right, towards the corridor, and they were able to see six pairs of bodyguards sticking to the walls standing at a distance of 5 meters each. The bodyguards were assigned to tight night security for a matter. A matter which was yet to be uncovered from them.

What was the matter?

And why was it so important that even some of the day bodyguards were assigned to give security at night?

Is the matter just being overhyped; or is it obvious because the danger degree indeed is very high? Whatever it was, the bodyguard must have forgotten that each suite has three private washrooms because he was so focused on giving the safety work. Based, on this the situation may have been of a higher degree.

'This is perfect.' Hannah was curious to know the A to Z of it while Hiroshi got confused about what was going on in life and wanted a cozy bed, not feeling sleepy anymore though.

On the other hand, the guards at the bar ordered some snacks to avoid looking suspicious. All the snacks were from different countries. One thing to remember is that they could get any continental food they want at any time. Snacks are nothing compared to that.

8 was recording them with utmost curiosity and interest because he was getting quality content. He was so satisfied, the best vlog he'd ever made! While giving voice delivery to the content, he realized that there was his favorite street food being served and started at its description- "Yeah guys so you can see that they are eating some Indian food right now. Some vegetables with some noodle-like thing; guys, oh my god, look at this. Oh my god!" But he didn't clearly mention what he was talking about. One of them, *the ostrich seeming,* had ordered 'भेल पूरी' (Bhel puri: an Indian street food; 8's favorite).

Randy came into the frame, doing the same thing, searching for 8 but was standing at a distance from the table this time. 8 was getting nervous and hungry seeing the ostrich eating his favorite Indian street food in front of him, some meters away. But at the same time, he was afraid of being caught by Randy's hands. But still lip-smack while seeing one of the bodyguards having the food.

Afraid of being caught in 4K.

Meanwhile the floor above:-

Hannah and Hirosh were worried. Hiroshi had to go to the washroom for nothing with another bodyguard in the name of safety.

Of course, he couldn't deny he was lying about going to the washroom.

That would be suspicious.

Back in the room both Hannah and Hiroshi made a plan to go out somehow. The plan was to use SISMO kits for going out since by that they could save themselves from being caught. Maintaining silence against the guards standing outside every suite door by the SISMO training!

Hiroshi was still insisting Hannah to let the matter be sorted by the bodyguards and the one who passed the order themselves but Hannah wouldn't listen. They both went to the corridor again and told the bodyguard that they have been called by Dominik. The bodyguard asked for proof. They both hesitated and went inside the room again. After appealing for some time the guard finally agreed but with the condition to go with a bodyguard. The bodyguard alloted FOR SAFETY PURPOSE was a long and thin woman. "Alright," Hannah had to agree to that and both went downstairs.

CHAPTER IX

The cocktail party inside the bar seems to end in eternity with all the time that passed, the intensity of the party increased even more. Three DJs have been changed from the start of the party. 8 was staring at the DJ while his recording was diverted to the primary personnel. The glass gate opens and a young female bodyguard enters. She was Asian. The *big man* who was sitting facing the glass gate signaled Dominik about it. "Oh, so you finally arrived! Come, have a seat."

"Oh my god, guys! Look. Something fishy's going on here. The girl came about whom Dom was talking. देख रही है सल्विया?(You're seeing it, Sylwia?)"

"I am sorry for being late sir. There was a minor concern at the helipad." Said Lumi the nighttime bodyguard.

"No worries. Provide 'Bella' with the details of the concern in the morning at 10:00. Now, since all of us are here, let's get to the business without any further due. Game of law." Dom passed a *'sadistic'* smile. (Not sure how else to put it)

'यहां हो क्या रहा है?' 8 was scarred at that look since he could realize that his personality changed with that very smile.

Personalities have been elaborated and described in the Upcoming novel cum manga ***DEAD BITE BY S.I.S.M.O.***

Also,

"Let's from now on call the thinner bodyguard as T'. That saves time since knowing his name would be of no profit. Still, since Abayomi's and Lumi's names have been exposed, we'll continue with the same."

Coming back:-

"S-so let's see what happens, next guys." He added to the dialogue and hesitated.'साला...'(A Hindi swear word) That swear word comes out of the fear he was experiencing deep inside him. Because, like most SISMO, Dom's personality is a dangerous one and 8 knew that very clearly. Once there was a dispute between fierce Randy and Dominik.

Let's save that story for some other day, shall we?

"Culprit can be here in a moment, we can't risk him getting away this time." T' said. *("What the hell is this ostrich talking about guys? Do you have any idea??" 8 asked into the camera from the darkness in the background.)*

"He's right. If the culprit appears here today then, that's our best chance to catch him. Sprang like a line on a prey."

"Do we have our positions defined, sir?" Asked Lumi.

"In a moment. I'll tell you that at the right time." Dom confirmed. *('What are they talking about? But it's fun.' 8 wondered.)*

On the other hand, Randy was satisfied that 8 isn't here anymore and he started enjoying the party again. Some bar girls approached him but he shouted at them and they walked away in annoyance. The three of them passed a glance at him with vexation. Randy doesn't care about girls if he's not interested.

"Let's start," Dom rose from his chair. "I think it's time to discuss our plans."

The guards glanced at him upwards.

8 was still recording in the dark corners.

<u>The plan-</u>

"I would be standing near the DJ on his left side. Lumi, I would like you to come with me and do as I say," (Personality) Dom said. "And when I said go, keep a record of my finger and move as I point.

I would be staring, observing, and taking note of everything in my mind. If anything unusual or to brood upon happens, we'll signal at each other and must understand it, (He licked his lips) That would be our signal. Don't take it otherwise; it's just for the people and rather for the intruder. He'll think that would think that we are picking up at some bar girl(s) for sure. As I'll like, when I suspect someone's body movements, I'll like you, Lumi, to walk to the dance floor, or maybe dancing would be better, I guess, and point at the man wherever he goes. I hope you have no problem?"

Lumi was shocked and didn't seem to like it, but she had to agree to the plan anyway.

She nodded timidly.

"Great! Bring the facts." Dom said with a wide sadistic smile again appeared.

"According to the observations, he's a pervert and a heavy drinker. He comes here every day and enjoys it till 6:00 in the morning. It almost feels like intruding is his part-time, but besides that, he entered the mansion. That proves that he's very clever to break our security system. And according to the law, he must be executed." T' confirmed to everyone.

"No. The news must not be proclaimed. I'll keep him in my prison. Great timing 'Ramzy,'" Said Dom. "For both, you guys must stick to the chair and please look relaxed to stay out of suspicion, right? Do you need girls?" (Dominik asked after a long pause)

At this statement, both males looked at each other but disagreed.

"Look, guys, they are talking about something, but we can't understand. But the guards look shocked." 8 was also recording all this.

"Well, I'll send them anyway. I can't believe that you could look normal at such a stage. Please cooperate." Dom confirmed with both of them and all set in their positions.

Meantime, Hiroshi and Hannah made it to the same floor and stood aside from the entrance. "What is happening? Why is Dom inside?" Hiroshi's eyes were wide open. "I don't know." Hannah shook her head and opened the door. The path was opened for them but immediately blocked by a bodyguard with a bulky body.

He was ordered for duty right now; blocking everyone to go in and out of the bar, except for the suspect. Along with the bodyguards, there were some policemen as well. Some policemen and more bodyguards are at a distance so that the people don't judge them for being with the police. Which they were.

"What are you doing ma'am?"

"What's happening? I want to know!"

CHAPTER X

"Ma‘am, actually... an intruder entered our premises." Said the bodyguard. "It happened a month while Dominik sir was abroad with his friends. When he heard of the trespassing a week ago, he hesitated and informed us to hold out on anyone about it. Then he started observing his movements every night, and today he's in the action with trusted bodyguards. Do you remember when the fancy dress party was held in Lily ma'am's and Herald sir's school? That's when the intruder broke into our mansion. According to our research and information, he is heading toward Bar-13. For eyeryboodie's security, we are sealing all the corridors too. He is very dangerous. I suppose you are aware of it, right?"

"Y-yeah-yeah." Hannah tried to appear as discreet as possible...

"You both should go back to your rooms. As fast as you can. He is insane. One thing of concern is that he might be carrying a weapon!" The bodyguard continued with a stern expression.

Hannah nodded her head and walked away with Hiroshi. But they were not going back. That was for sure; after knowing the thing that had been kept hidden from them for a long time.

"Now what?" Started Hiroshi after they left the bar far behind and the music faded.

"I don't know," Hannah answered in a low voice.

"What do you mean you don't know? You messed my precious sleep for a silly adventure!" Hiroshi started to pule. Hannah frowned. But she lift her chin and started back at Hiroshi.

"Shut up Hiroshi! I have to save my brother!" She yelled at him.

"He is going to face a psychopath alone! I have to save him from that psycho. If sleep is of more importance to you then you may go! I can handle this alone."

"Okay-okay, I am sorry. I understand but...what are you going to do now?" Said Hiroshi after a pause.

'And what about 8?'

He understood her emotions. She mitigated that he understood.

She started pondering upon a smarter move to surpass the bodyguards at his statement. While moving, she walked past the kitchenette on the left. Suddenly, her view fell upon the vent.

"Hiroshi," she said and Hiroshi looked at her on the left. "I know what to do. We can save Dom now." Hannah's mood lifted and she gave an eye smile.

CHAPTER XI

At first, Hiroshi thought that, or it felt like, Hannah was being moody for not leaving everything to the bodyguards, but it was her **SISMO personality.**

"What?" Asked Hiroshi.

Hannah pointed towards the ceiling with her constant smile.

"The vent?" Questions flooded through his expressions.

"Yeah! We can go through the vent!" She was filled with enthusiasm like she had achieved something big. The thing was that the vent was open with no one inside the kitchenette. Hannah planned to go through the vent into the bar.

Hiroshi gulped and nodded. They tried hard for some time but were ultimately unsuccessful. That was at quite a height.

Inside the club, 8 was still on the ground in the same pose, still recording the scenario. The paper seeming one and Big Ryan were with girls. The girls were looking happy with them. Lumi was standing in her position. Dominik started talking with her in sign language. Lumi gave a thumbs-up and started dancing in a weird manly way. Her expression was straight and didn't change at all while she was feeling *death by shyness* inside of her soul. Suddenly Randy's eyes crashed on Lumi. He saw her dancing. Her dancing wasn't that good it was a hell of an absurd.

"रे," 8's eyes opened wide. He started spicing up the situation. "Yoyoyo guys! As you can see, this is what happens in rich people's houses; mansions. They even want to see their bodyguards dance! As you can see Dominik J. Santorski gave a sign to that poor little bodyguard whose parents are so poor to feed her and she became a bodyguard under him because she was good for nothing. Now being a bodyguard she has to dance because there's nothing she could do for now! Poor, poor gal. देख रही है सिल्विया?(You're seeing it, Sylwia?)"

Randy walked to the dance floor and started-

"Ha! Ha! Ha! Lumi, what's up with that style? Haa!"

"..." She continued her dangerous dance. She swang her arm in the air, and Randy escaped the blow by just an inch.

"That's not correct. Come I'll teach you how to dance." A smirk on his face.

"..."

"Don't care to answer, huh?" Continued Randy while she, seemed to have a blind eye upon him, went on throwing her arms and legs in the air like crazy.

"Aye, you gone nuts! I may have been hurt."

"..."

"Okay, okay! If you don't want then I'll leave." Randy left the dance floor and sat on his seat again. Dominik was looking at Lumi. She realizes that Randy was also there. *'Now, where the hell did he come from..!'* She thought. Meanwhile, the other two bodyguards were talking to the girls and enjoying themselves, but they weren't feeling comfortable at all in reality as it wasn't their work. While 8 was recording all this with interest as he was getting great content.

INSIDE THE KITCHENETTE:-

Hannah and Hiroshi were still struggling with the vent.

"It's too high. It'll take forever."

"Hmmm, isn't there a ladder around?"

"It's your mansion, Hannah! How could I know the details of your house?"

"My mansion's too big to understand and my brain's too small..."

"Is this a time to joke?!" Hiroshi was much more serious this time.

"Alright, alright. Let me think." Hannah rubbed her chin as an expression to think. The whole area was quiet as death. "Yes!" Hannah broke the silence with the exclaim. This spontaneous expression shocked Hiroshi but never the less he asked what.

"Kneel! I'll climb over you and after that, I'll use my ***gravity block*** technique to climb up on my own and finally into the vent." She said with the same sarcastic smile.

"And what about me, huh?"

"Ummm, I'll think. Wait..."

"What the hell!" Hiroshi was annoyed with her childish expressions.

Subsequently, Hiroshi said- "Hannah,"

"Yes?"

"Let's carry out with the first plan."

"But what about you?"

"We'll see about that. I think I have a plan." He replied calmly.

CHAPTER XII

They again started to think something. That plan was a flop.

"So?" Hiroshi was panting.

"You can't lift me?"

"I don't wanna break my back. You're too heavy."

"Shut up Hiroshi," Hannah boasted.

"I am only 50kgs!"

"Doesn't looks so..." He chuckled.

"Shut up, again."

"Should *I* climb on you? Because I don't think this is working. You're small." Hiroshi said after a pause.

"What? No! Isn't there any other way??"

"Can *you* think of something?" Hiroshi asked as if he was so tired now mixed with some aggression.

"Okay, just leave it." Said Hannah after a long pause and sighed.

Party was still going on in the bar. Randy was still trying to teach Lumi how to dance but the reply was only being an ultimate level of ignorance and silence by her side. After trying several times to talk, Randy in the end finally gave up. "Fine, you don't wanna learn? That's fine." He said and went back to the table.

Till now it was around 2:56 AM. Big man's bar girl slept upon his chest while T''s was drinking heavily and laughing loudly.

Enjoying the party.

They (the bodyguards) talked in sign language:-

"Do you really think he'll come? Ramzy?"

"According to the reports, it is most likely, but not a hundred percent guaranteed."

"We just have to wait till 6:00 in the morning. But it is still three hours to go."

"My back hurts. I've been sitting too long."

"But we'll catch him this time. (Abayomi was not in a mood to wonder about something else except for the case being) *I am not letting it out. Not only because I want to become the leader of all the bodyguards and earn all the five stars but also to remove this intruder because this is my workplace!"*

"That was so mutual. But I'll get all five stars before you. Currently, I am at three already."

At that moment a waitress crosses by their table, passing a smile. They gave forced smiles as well to look more natural.

"Hey! What is this man?! We are not here to discuss our bodyguard matters! Do you understand? We'll discuss it sometime later."

"O-Ok, sorry."

"But still, I will be the one to get them all before you..." Says Big man after a pause.

T' gives him a pathetic eye glance.

> *"The stars Abayomi and T' were talking about is the grading system for each bodyguard. The more ranks they earn the more stars they get as an achievement. Being a total number of five, mostly most of the bodyguards are not even able to get close to three stars. The one with the four stars badge is already considered a conqueror since it is a really tough job to get each one of them.*

Currently, only one bodyguard possesses all the five stars. The one with the eye patch. But we'll talk about her in some other episode, shall we? That girl has a different story(Spoiler)."

8 had started to get dizzy now. The fact that the place was warm and he was laying on the ground. That proved to be a cherry on the top condition to dose off in.

'अब मुझे क्या करना चाहिए? मैं सो जाऊँ क्या?' (What should I do now? Go to sleep?)

Ultimately the bar started to get emptier as the bodyguards were aware that they have to serve their duties as a bodyguard from 7:00 in the morning. The remaining including the one with the mission can be counted on fingers.

'Should I go too?' Randy too started to feel the same. *'Not so fast.'* He smirked since he was enjoying himself so much.

At 2:00- Finally, from the glass door, an elderly-looking man with skinny cheeks and clothes over a skeletal body entered. Badly shaved grey beard, partially bald, pooping yellow eyes, suffering from ptosis with the left one. Bent and had extreme overbite teeth. Looking kinda tired. Dominik's eyes caught him by his body language the moment he entered. He licked his upper lip but Lumi wasn't aware. She wasn't looking. He tried two more times and on the last try, her line of sight fell and she understood the gesture.

Her moves changed.

She started pointing to the man moving around the bar. Now with less than ten people, it could be clearly seen.

8's eyes followed the bent, old man too since he looked so different from the people he ever saw inside the mansion.

"Whoa, look," Started Abayomi with a normal tone as his eyes fell and followed up on the old new commer. "That must be him. Uh..?"

"Let's start with the real business," Says T', with a very stern expression, pointing a gun at Abayomi. "Shall we, *Big Man?*" He passes a cruel smile.

CHAPTER XIII

Come on camera; Unfiltered. 8's youtube channel. 8 has a vlogging channel where he vlogs as well as motivates people to start showing themselves to the world with no makeup or filter. According to him, filters are like demons that hide your true face. Take it as an angel, behind a beautiful but deadly lie in the form of a filter, and a filter as a demonic disguise. Like Hannah and all, he believes that natural faces with marks, blemishes, and even wrinkles are true beauty that is much more beautiful than cosmetic and plastic faces used to hide them. Because of this many of his subscribers and close ones also started to embrace their true beauty even more and because of this reason, he is among the most liked YouTubers in the world. But remember, he's a vlogger too. *The channel's for vlogging too.*

Coming back to the episode:-

"Ramzy! I...Is this supposed to be some kind of a joke!? What are you doing?" Abayomi couldn't figure out the behavioral change that just T' showed him.

He was just joking, wasn't he?

"I don't have time for little, worthless chit-chats anymore! Take me to the prison. And once we get out, don't try to act smart. It will be good for you and for all of us. You don't want anybody inside to be hurt because of you, do you??" T' said with a very stern and serious expression, still pointing the gun.

"You think you could get away with this!?" Abayomi stood up while looking at the gun pointed at him.

"I'll be right behind you. Once we are out, one smart trick and I'll voice activate the dynamite inside this bar. (Abayomi's wondered in fear; not for himself but for the mansion) You don't want to kill everyone inside, especially your respected boss Dominik do you?" He passes a much cunning smile to him. Abayomi's hands were bound to do what T' was telling him to just because of the hi-tech weapon. They normally started to move out. What the hell suddenly happened to him?!!

He isn't the intruder, right?

RIGHT?!!

Meanwhile, 8 dozed off to a sound sleep.

Lumi was still pointing at the new man who entered while dancing. Dom liked his lower lip, telling her to stop the action and to sit at some table. The weird new man went to two bar girls and started dancing with both of them, standing between them.

For Randy, he observed all of this; what Lumi and Dom did, what happened between Big man and T' and this weird old man. He now knew that something wasn't normal with what was going on in here.

That was something fishy.

Something really very turmoil going on.

Lumi comes and sits next to Randy. Her straight expression, as ever, turned more intense now.

"What are you doing here Randy?" She started without turning her head.

"That's what I am supposed to know first. What's going on here!? Why didn't you talk to me? Why Dominik is here? Why Ramzy pointed a gun at Abayomi? And whose this weird man you were pointing at!?"

Lumi took a pause for a second. In shock, she finally turned to him- "Ramzy pointed a gun at Abayomi?!" Randy observed Lumi's eyes grow wider as she removed her glasses slowly.

The DJ was playing slow party music now. The weird man was dancing with them both. He was rubbing their waists so impulsively that the bar girls weren't liked and they were continuously removing his hands. He was also sticking his face to their chests since he was their chest height. The girls were resisting these critical things so much. That was pure harassment that was **strictly** framed against the rules of the bars. The resentment for the man's sinful actions could be clearly seen in the girls' body language. The pervert now started at the girl's neck on the left side with his thin, wrinkled hand. He puts the hand behind the girl's head and kisses her. Suddenly.

The girl finally openly jerked the man backward with a loud cry.

"Now!"

At Dom's order everyone i.e. all the left bodyguards, bar girls, waiters, and even the DJ pointed guns against him.

"WHAT WAS THAT BEHAVIOUR YOU BITC-" He stops as he observes that everyone inside the bar has pointed arms against him. Even the bar girls he was dancing with had guns pointing directly at the back of his head. He got so fuzzed up. Right then, 8 woke up from his sleep and witnessed the intended condition. '*What the-*' His eyes were wide and when he glanced down he saw that the recording was still on while he had been in dreams. But he was now shivering, scared by the turmoil happenings. What could have gone wrong in the mean five minutes while *I* was sleeping? That was his/an obvious question.

"Tell us your motive! One of the two intruders! Broke into our security system easily and entered in the month of December 2021! Last week. Drop any weapon that you might be carrying and surrender!! Your subordinate will be caught before daylight! On your knees, NOW!" Directed the **DJ** from the stage to the pervy old man.

As the man turns to look, observation was that literally, everyone had arms. Against him! He hesitates when he gains the sense to understand the perfect planning that got him to the present and then bursts into peals of laughter. "Well, then it's plan E that'll take place now." He says afterward.

8 was so shocked at the unexplainable sudden changes. But vlogging gave him some comfort so he continued recording. Only a vlogger knows the emotions. He knew that he could easily get away from the place because of his training but he wanted to know more about all that mess happening.

Randy saw everyone to be in the same offensive position against the weird man while he was still sitting in the corner chair.

"Now that you know everything (that I just told you and that you heard yourself), should you need the invitation to get in position?" Lumi says to him who was pointing the gun as well.

"B-But I don't have a gun..." He says.

"Tsk, this man. I have a gun in my back pocket. Just take it."

"Huh, what-" Randy hesitated. He couldn't touch a girl like that. It was the pocket at the back she was talking about. Lumi after seeing his approach to the advice took the gun out herself and gave it to him.

"Now all we need to do is to follow sir Dominik's words." She again says without turning her head.

"Thanks!" Randy points the gun at the man too.

"Plan E? No wonder you must have made a lot of plans in the past to get in," said Dominik nonchalantly. "Just go ahead, do it then."

That led to confusion in the minds of the guards. His expression fell into confusion.

Why was Dominik so cool about the plan he didn't know existed?

"You're so cool, huh?" The man says. "I don't believe you have a bit of idea about the degree of danger involved."

"I would like to see the danger you could put me in."

From now on, we'll call the old man *Mujrim.*

In a moment, the mujrim was nastier through his actions now. Seeing that Dominik was so cool about the plan bugged him even more. "!أنت لا تعرف شيئًا تزحف إليه" He said in Arabic, *'You don't know a thing you creep!'*

"Talking in Arabic, huh? So, you *are* a Dubai citizen. Looks like you aren't afraid of the outcomes of your crimes then."

"!لا على الإطلاق" Said Mujrim with more grudge in his voice which means *'Not at all!'* "لم أكن لأفعل ذلك في المقام الأول إذا شعرت بالخوف" *'I wouldn't have done it in the first place if I was to be scared.'*

"Well, okay then. Get the job done already." Dom was still nonchalant with an adamant mindset (personality) while Randy realized for the first time that Dominik could understand Arabic.

"You're seeing this Lumi?" He whispered. "Sir can understand the language."

"We all can. Wait can't you understand Arabic??" She replied and asked.

Randy returned his head direction without answering. *Bad impression.*

"I am waiting. Do it. Or are you scared? Believe me, I don't even know a tad about it."

"Tch!" His grimace deepened. There was clear fury in his eyes. Fire crossed his mind.

"You don't seem so fastidious about your own so-called 'plan E', you know?" Dominik was enjoying...

Meanwhile, 8 was still recording with much interest.

"DON'T BE SO BOAST OF YOURSELF! I COULD TRIGGER IT, YES, ONLY I CAN!"

"Sir, this isn't looking okay, shall we finish it once and for all?" Asks one of the waiters with the gun.

"Even if this man maves a finger just shoot him," Dom commands them all. "Now you are being nasty by not doing what you're supposed to," Dom continued the nonchalant speech to the mujrim, ignoring the danger.

"أنت...! (You...!)" The man lost words to show aggression.

"If you can't entertain me any further, listen to this now- I know that you've just been used by your own subordinate, your son who has disguised as Ramzy T. Joy, one of my *gatekeeper* cum guards to break in easily and accomplish your design. Now I also know that you've disabled all the cameras in your line of the path where you were trying to make the plan execution after breaking in. You waited for some time in the public washroom to observe the working inside of this mansion. That went on for seven days straight in the last month, after which your son disguised himself as the guard while you as a normal employee working under our business. That gave both the knowledge about the nature of work and working conditions inside the mansion. Whatever your plan might be, I know you lack the confidence to do it without your son's companionship. And by the way, I also am aware that you've been dominated by your own son in your crimes, you're just a pawn while your son thinks himself to be the bishop if there are none in the outer world conducting your mission. Maybe the king himself...*I don't mind that*... But, somewhere, inside of you you envy your own son because you think your experience in this field is much more widespread than that of your son, but then he uses force isn't it? Now that feeling took the form of haterade, isn't it true? That proves that you're in this crime business for quite a while now... And just like you put several weapons around, I too kept my faithful guards with me. That's it, argue if you can on this matter..."

Listening to the reality about the relation, which was only a hypothesis by Dominik, the mujrim showered in sweat and was struck by a deep fear-filled feeling of being busted by some professional. He had already started to see the ending of all of this. He knew that only the *'plan E'* would work now.

WHAT WAS THE PLAN?

"You aren't responding. Does that prove my deduction to be in the right direction? It's indeed in reality then... I know your whole crime design in a much more bright light, but it will take the whole night to be explained. At one point I really appreciate your planning but-" Just as Dominik was about to continue, and the mujrim gritted his overbite teeth, the vent started with some thump and throb sounds. Everyone stared at the vent. But Dom still kept his eyes stuck on the mujrim. In a moment the sounds became more obvious. That was so unnatural that some of the guards had to point their guns at the vent as well. "Who's in there?!" Yelled one of the guards.

No reply.

And the thumpings died as well.

Dom walks a bit closer to the vent with his hands under his pockets. "Say it already or we're gonna shoot anyway." But his eyes were still stuck on mujrim who was gazing at him with a stern expression in return.

"Dominik!" Said the voice. "Are you alright? It's me."

"Hiroshi!?"

Just at that moment seeing that Dominik and all moved their focus from him, the mujrim hijacked the bargirl he harassed a while ago with a pistol on her temple. She shrieked and the focus turned back onto him. And just at that very moment Hiroshi and Hannah fell from the vent to the ground.

"I've already broken into your security system! Now I know all your secrets and-" Shreaked mujrim back to him but Dom bumped in between his statement with a nonchalant '*Shut up*'.

'*आखिरी आज रात हो क्या रहा है?!*' Thought 8. '*ये कैसी साल की शुरुआत हुई है?*' (What the hell's going on tonight?! What start of the year has this been?)

CHAPTER XIV

Everybody was clearly confused. **Literally, literally everyone.**

Shit! Shit! SHIT!

"If you wanna shoot, (continued Dominik and made a gun from his left hand pointing directly at mujrim), then do it ASAP. I don't have all the time in the world."

"Sir... What are you saying?" The bar girl said as if she would burst into tears right away. Her companion got chills too. But the expression of the mujrim was much noticeable. His expression went as down as possible for him to do. He was in a great dilemma by Dom's behavior. In fact, the guards were in shock too about what was Dominik thinking!?

"Don't worry Lumi," Said Randy in a low voice to Lumi after seeing her confused expression. "I know what the ending might look like..." He smirked.

"..." Clear muddeling mind.

With a fierce expression, as the bar girl cried for help, the mujrim turned the gun from her and shot Dominik in the head...

CHAPTER XV

Abayomi leads T‘ to a dark corridor with black matt colored walls and a shiny black sliding door at the end of the hallway. They stop in front of the same door. "That’s the secret prison, isn’t it?" Asks T’ gravely.

Abayomi nods in dejection. But that brings an eerie grin to T‘’s face instead. His smile fades and he moves his head while pointing the gun at the big man’s temple. Telling him to open it for him. As the gate opens, Abayomi opens it, it turns the condition like an hourglass. It was time for Abayomi’s smile. Several heavy-suited bodyguards, behind the gate with arms, point their guns against T’.

"What the hell?!"

"Traitor," starts Abayomi calmly turning back at him. "You aren’t real Ramzy T.J. are you? If you were then you would have known that there is heavy security outside the bar." He continues with a smirk on his face.

T' grits his teeth and tries to voice activate the dynamite but one of the guards shoots the machine from his hand, breaking it into pieces. Then in an attempt to escape once and for all, he tries to shoot himself but the bullet doesn’t come out from his gun. Heavily suited bulky men catch him. Finally, he got handcuffed while Abayomi was still smirking down at him.

At the bar, all of that was being recorded: ***All of that was recorded.***

There was just the trigger’s sound.

No bullet came out.

"Whoa, you just made my stomach full of butterflies..." Dominik smiled normally. Teasingly.

Mujrim's eyes, as a ball of drool followed by a thinner line dripped from the left end of his thin, brown lips, popped out in wonder and he showered in even more salty, smelly sweat. The bar girl and the mujrim were both surprised, and their hearts pounding in their chests like they would jump out. He tried three-four more times but he ultimately knew it was his end.

That he was so busted.

After realizing that his plan failed to kill everyone inside with the dynamite he felt a cold hand on his left shoulder. As he turned back he saw a girl with a blank expression, wide-eyed, staring down at him. That look increased the intensity of the chill that zig-zagged his spine at that moment even more.

"Your chance is over," said Hannah and gave him a full blow of knuckles on his face and he fell with blood splashed from his face with two yellow molars and a cry, removing the hand from the hostage's neck and knocking the empty gun off from the other hand.

• • •

"Luca," Said Dominik to the bar girl. "You have the right to get 10,000 Hungarian Forint as compensation for the assault as per your contract."

She nodes.

"Plus," he continues. "You also have the right to thrash that intruder. But concerning his age, it would only last for five minutes."

"Thanks, sir. But I don't want to see his face ever again. You're gonna put him in your prison, that's enough revenge for me."

"What? Well, that's fine too. Happy that you'll continue to work." He says with a smile.

The girl, Luca, smiles, and leaves with her companion. Hannah and Hiroshi now knew everything that the matter was about. Randy realized that he was invited too for the mission but because he left earlier **that night** he didn't hear it from his boss. Paige was ill so she couldn't come. (One more personal bodyguard; main role in the Dead Bite)

8 (or Shreyance; if you forgot) understood everything too but he was still in his hiding spot, disguised from them all. He was too scared to come out now.

"To all my bodyguards- Like I've already told you that the mission would end before 3:00 AM. Look... it's 2:59 clock. I always keep my promises, thank me later. Now, in this mansion. In *our* mansion even the door knobs are hi-tech," Dom continues from bodyguards to the mujrims. "What were you thinking that you could pass the surveillance system? I was always right. My argument with Alice (elder sister; in case you forgot) to put hidden cameras *inside* the surveillance cameras was all right after all."

Hannah nods. She was also during that discussion with Dom and Alice.

"Even if the lock of a door breaks there are still two hidden ones to take its place. At this rate, a surveillance system is a big deal." Dom says to both the intruders tied with blindfolds and gagged like they have been kidnapped.

"Even the door knobs are hi-tech." Starts Hannah.

"That's what I just said."

Hannah smiles.

"From the hidden surveillance camera boss along with us always kept an eye on your actions from the day we observed something strange happening." Said Abayomi.

"Since I observed your behavior, I could see where both of you used to keep your outfit material. And for the guns, I did away with the bullets. And that's the reason I've already done away with the dynamite to Dubai police before arriving at today's meeting as well. That's what I was doing while Randy, you were telling me something. I was messaging the local police about the matter of concern. (Randy was shocked at hearing this, but then his respect for Dominik grew even more in his mind.) Also, by seeing your approach to each other it was easily deducible that you had a father-son relationship. Also that your father held some haterade against that bossy behavior of yours."

Hiroshi swallowed after hearing this. (Read the **Trillionaire's Night Ride** to know why.)

Hannah gazed at his and stifled a laugh on this.

"The real Ramzy is still unaware of the presence of a copy of him inside our mansion with a completely different motive for our second home." Says one of the female guards with three stars. The one who was allotted for Hiroshi and Hannah.

"Thanks," Says Dominik to the bodyguard very nonchalantly. "I just happened to slip that part. You, *fake Ramzy Tailor Joy*, really did a good job in keeping your real self secretive, but it is said that *a big plan fails due to small mistakes,* (In the meantime everybody moves their heads at each other, even 8 wonders; we haven't heard such a phase. But okay...) you missed that the real Ramzy has a cut upon his left eyebrow and three small pimple marks on the same side, one on his head and the rest upon his cheekbone. I never knew what your plan E was, but frankly speaking, I over-smarted it without knowing anything about it."

Just as he moves both the mujrims start to move their bodies and make statements through the gag like they wanted to say something.

The waiter from the left, disguised guard exclaims at him, telling him to stop it, they aren't going to let them speak. But Hannah says that they are *visitors*. We can't stop them from sharing their words. On Hannah's indirect order, one guard unties their mouth.

"HAHAHAHAHAHA!," Starts the son in an utterly maniacal, or like a psycho, manner. "YOU THINK YOU'VE WON! This plan was on my side from the start, you see that أب (Father)!? PLAN 'E' WORKED! WE ARE NOT GONNA LEAVE THIS PLACE ALIVE, سوف نموت! انا سعيد جدا. (We're gonna die! I am so happy.) أترى هذا الرجل العجوز ؟! هل ترى؟ عملت خطتنا. انا اكثر من سعيد! (You see this old man?! Do you see? Our plan worked. I AM MORE THAN HAPPY!)" In the end, he praises his holy God.

One thing to remember is that all the Arabic lines flew away for Randy, Hannah, and Hiroshi as they don't understand a bit of the language.

"ばかも. (Stupid)" Says Hiroshi after a pause. One bodyguard translated everything in his ear.

"Not so fast," Starts Hannah. "You think your gonna get away so easily? Don't you know that it is a SISMO's mansion you've tried to execute the plan into?" At this statement, their eyes popped with a huge shock.

S-SISMO!!??!

NOW it was all over. It was known...

"Son. I've always told you this was a bad idea..." Says the father to the son.

Dom starts with the final nonchalant statements to the mujrims before they will be taken to his prison- "Your son's too just like you Mr, whatever your name is. (I'll look into that sometime later anyway) He speaks without even thinking and laughs very loudly without caring about his surrounding. That proves he hasn't attended school after 3rd or 4th grade, isn't it? This is the behavior I've observed with people like him. Believe me, I didn't have a tad about your plan when you forced the gun on the lady's head. I am still telling you that. I just used your anger to make you do some mistakes and being adamant really worked. I was successful but your son was a lot easier to be caught because of his foolish boastful behavior. I might have been shot. But I knew how to do things to the best. It's just a SISMO experience nothing else. So, weren't my plans more fastidious? Am I allowed to laugh like a psycho now? (He supposed but he controlled that laugh somehow) Since being a SISMO I have permission from the Dubai police, now you'll be, both of you, kept under my prison and won't be left until you become the man I am supposed, *a S.I.S.M.O.'s supposed,* to be making you! That's why I told you everything. Because you arn't escaping this mansion before twenty years anymore now." He finished with a much more dominant voice than the whole time in the end.

• • •

"Your little, finicky *Plan E* didn't work after all, huh?" Lumi wanted to take out her grudge (that is some other matter; not related to this episode) so she teased the mujrims while they were being tied in straight jackets, to be taken easily to the prison.

"You liked a disguised game, didn't you? Look, Dominik, my buddy, took inspiration from you. Ha ha ha!" Hiroshi rosed a joke against the two mujrims as well while they were being carried to the prison.

"For the next 20 years, you won't be freed..." Says Hiroshi after a pause, rather slowly this time looking at the mujrims who've already been taken away.

"To all of you," started the police commissioner to all the bodyguards exept than Abayomi and Lumi for the mission. "It would be of great pleasure for me to promote you with one additional star! As per Dominik sir's and Hannah ma'am's granting the opportunity; I would be the one to do the pleasure with my own hands at 12:00 in the afternoon." He continued.

One of the happiest moments for all the one and two-star guards!

Meanwhile,

Hiroshi- "What would you rate this terrorist mission, Dominik?"

Dominik- "Huh? How should we do it, Hannah? Well-"

Randy- "Rating reminds me of a bad boy, by the way."

Hannah from nowhere- "Oh yeah! What about 8?"

Randy with a little wonder- "How did you know that I was talking about 8, Hannah ma'am?"

Hiroshi- "Huh?!"

Dominik- "Oh, he?" Dom takes them to the same chair on which they were sitting earlier and removes the curtain behind it. "Here." He points 8 who was busted by Dominik as well and he looks at them with wide fearful eyes, fearing only for Randy since he's furious because of 8. His phone battery- Dead, the place he put it in- Under his pocket.

"You're here!?"

"Eh, sorry Rando for doing that earlier..." He was shivering.

"8! Uncle! What are you doing here?" Hannah asks with excitement.

"Wait, doing *what* with Randy?" Asks Hiroshi.

"Uh, nothing..." Randy discards the idea as he didn't want to make a bad impression again. But through his green eyes, he already had warned 8 that he won't forgive him. "But sir, *you* hid this m...(He controlled the swear word from slipping his mouth) *b-boy*, behind the curtains?"

"Eh...?"

"No Randy," Dom answers. "I saw him drinking water in the kitchen some hours ago while I was about to leave the suite for this very mission. I tried to run past while he wasn't looking but, seems I should have waited a bit longer instead. When I entered the corridor I saw his big nose, hiding behind a white flower vase table. I thought he hadn't followed me seeing that I was in the bar. But I remembered his behavior after that. He's controversial, not only with us but on the internet too and you know that. Yes, I deduced he was following me. So I wasn't surprised seeing him going in and from the washroom. And Randy followed him in anger so he hid behind the curtains. And from that point on he was constantly behind the curtains. *Disguised* just like the nature of the case today's night. I just decided not to disturb him, that's all."

8 was more shocked than what he saw throughout the night.

"I just wanted to know what you were doing late at night. You know?" 8 replied.

"There's no wonder he came here to create a *mess*. That's it." Said Randy gravely.

"Shut up, mad." 8 shivered after saying what he shouldn't have. Randy raged at him and was almost about to punch him.

Hiroshi- "Randy just leave him."

8- "Yeah leave me...(scared)"

Hiroshi happily- "We'll beat him together the next day."

8- "Wait, WTF bro?"

Randy and Hiroshi passed high fives. Hannah and Dominik laugh at that sudden logical tactic.

8 annoyed but finally asks Randy something when he remembers- "Hey, Randy boy. What are you doing in *this* bar anyway?" Everyone stopped laughing.

"Oh, yeah. That's what I thought too. I just forgot about that. Why is it, Randy?"

"Uh, sir... (Randy peeks at Lumi's seat) It was... uh, just... because I had some fight with someone. (He lied)"

"Why are you always fighting?!" Hannah asked seriously.

"Sorry, ma'am."

"You don't need to use the word ma'am every time." She says really quietly so that no one could hear.

They talked more while going back to the suite when while talking 8 reveals that he had recorded everything on his phone that had happened inside from the start. Dominik was shocked that he was recording everything since that was rated as SSZZZ. He hurriedly asks for the recording-

"Where is the recording?!!"

"I didn't do anything with the video." He said with wide eyes like he didn't want to tell anything. "I just shared it on the friend's group, shared it with Mr. and Mrs. Santorski (Dom's parents), Alice, and posted it on the internet."

"YOU DID WHAT!?" Dom was shocked for the first during the whole time.

[illegible] and Hiroshi passed high fives. [illegible] at that sudden logical move.

[illegible] usually asks Randy something [illegible] Hey, Randy [illegible] What are you doing? [illegible] Everyone stopped laughing.

[illegible] That [illegible] I thought I just forgot [illegible]

[illegible] because I had some fight with someone. (He [illegible])

[illegible] always [illegible] He [illegible]

S.I.S.M.O. is a secret group of people around the World.

"S.I.S.M.O. existed from the start of human civilization. Over the last three centuries, there have been many disappearances of criminals. At their retrieval, most of the criminals became completely changed men, who served society and helped in convincing everyone to follow ethical life and lived a more radiant life ever since. While those criminals who remained adamant about the training were never seen again. Evil is better off dead.

Don't you think so?

It is a secret group that only those who are the members know exactly about and any random individual can't tell if the person standing in front of him is a Sismo or not.

They are not like a terrorist group or dark web users, but rather 'agents' who are chosen from the public itself by other Sismos who believe that a particular man/woman chosen can be a new member of the Sismo group or community as well.

The people chosen as Sismo live normally like every other person, but he must hide his Sismo identity from everyone else(since it can only be known to another Sismo.) And at times when they are called by the higher authority (whom they call 'BOSS'), they must retire from their work at the present and must report to the place allocated to them by those higher authorities on time, which is usually in cafes or parks or just by the roadsides or at any public place. This helps in keeping their identities personal and unnatural.

They are assigned different missions and based on the level or degree of danger and importance the members are selected based on their long years of training and brain-boosting to solve the matter while being fair to the government and Laws.

Sismos are among those secrets of the government that are kept hidden by them from the normal public, like alien sightings.

They are spread all over the World and work for the welfare of the people and especially they are so bound that they can't talk about being a sismo to family members. Their ways are different however, they might kill you too if they feel that you are just like a burden on society. But that's not so obvious. They'll try to make you an efficient and higher-valued person in any way possible. Hence their ways of thinking are different from normal people's as well.

But that doesn't mean they are bad people anyway. Rather right. Many hate them calling their deeds cruel murder but it's not like that.

All the characters presented to you are SISMOs themselves! And that's why we are defining the SISMOs for you.

Everything else about a SISMO group and its history (how it started) will be revealed in our new upcoming novel, DEAD BITE, available shortly."

“*Stay tuned!*”

Take a photo (on the next page) and put it on your social media with the mention to support our effort⇒ ThatNightSISMO

For instagram⇒ TeamINVINCIBLES

THAT NIGHT

also

S.I.S.M.O. 14+

presents

DEAD

BITE

ANIME BASED

By the creaters of MUTEKI NO BUNTAI y/t

Help us go trending before the release of our manga cum novel with the hashtag #DeadBiteSISMO or #DeadBitebySISMO

If you like this book then, please take a moment to donate some money to the writer and his team ⬇

(You can also do it by the method below for free.)

Follow our YouTube Channel for the latest updates; Become a member of our group/ family by subscribing!

@mutekiNoBuntai23

or

Scan to go.

9 798889 518204

Printed by Libri Plureos GmbH in Hamburg, Germany